pseud Aquila

The Passing of the Poet

And other Poems

pseud Aquila

The Passing of the Poet
And other Poems

ISBN/EAN: 9783337398088

Printed in Europe, USA, Canada, Australia, Japan

Cover: Foto ©Andreas Hilbeck / pixelio.de

More available books at **www.hansebooks.com**

THE

PASSING OF THE POET

AND OTHER POEMS

By AQUILA

LONDON
KEGAN PAUL, TRENCH, TRÜBNER, & CO. L^TD
PATERNOSTER HOUSE, CHARING CROSS ROAD
1893

DEDICATION.

To VEGA.

From AQUILA.

THE patient-eyed Aquila,* night by night,
  Looks with eternal love, that cannot die,
  Up to his radiant Queen, enthroned on high,—
His ever-smiling Vega, angel bright,
Who dwells beyond his reach, in Heaven's height.
  O happy love ! that lives without a sigh,
  Awaiting happier days that may be nigh ;—
A consummation hoped for is delight.

But my belovéd Vega long has set :
  With heart, and soul, and life, I watch in vain :—
The afterglow, undying, lingers yet ;
  But I shall never see my Queen again.
O my beloved ! wherefore hast thou flown,
To leave me with these lesser stars alone ?

---

* The three leading stars of Aquila point in a line up to Vega *for ever.*

CONTENTS.

CONTENTS

THE PASSING OF THE POET.

" Ages past the soul existed,
 Here an age 'tis resting merely."
 —BROWNING.

*It is midnight.   The Poet is asleep in his chamber,
    with his head bowed down and resting on his arms
    upon the table.   The night is clear.   The light
    from a crescent moon streams in through the open
    window, and the stars look down upon the earth.
    Close by the window stands an astronomical
    telescope.   On the table lie scattered books, papers,
    and star maps, and the last sonnet which the Poet
    has written.**

SONNET.

*THE BLIND ASTRONOMER.

THY mind to me was like the deep, blue sky,
    Thy thoughts the stars I studied with a hope
    Beyond belief.   Love was my telescope.
I watched their motions with a faithful eye,
In silent hours, when no one else was nigh :
    Until a door was shut I could not ope,

A

And darkness came, with which I could not cope ;
Then from the task I sank, with weary sigh.
Now, like a poor astronomer struck blind,
Through the dark silence of the night and day,
In patient occultation of the mind,
I wait for God's own hand to roll away
The mist, that hides the glory of the skies,
And lift the veil of darkness from mine eyes.

(*The Poet dreams, and speaks in his sleep.*)

POET.

Ye living spirits, that inhabited
The dust of those that here have sinned and sung :
Eternal souls, that for a season made
A dwelling place in forms of flesh and blood,
Creating man—a wondrous, living thing,
With hopes and fears, ambition and despair ;
Ye souls, that did endow the beating hearts
With pain, and passion, and emotions strange,
Where! where do ye abide?   Where is the light
That glimmered in those eyes, long since consigned
To Death's eternal night?   And where
The fount of music, and the source of song?

(*A spirit appears to him.*)

Beautiful being ! Godlike in thy form !
To whom existence seemeth a delight,
Whence comest thou ?   And wherefore art thou come ?

SPIRIT.

Mortal, from regions where the whirling spheres
In beauty circle round unnumbered suns
In swift descent, outspeeding light, I come!
Sent hither by the Great Omnipotent,
Who ruled before all time, and as He ruled
Without beginning, so without an end
Will rule, Eternal! Awful! Infinite!
Of whom to think bewilders mortal minds.
And I am here to guide thine erring soul,
And point thee out the path that thou must take.

POET.

O radiant envoy of the King of Kings!
Here, in the presence of thy loveliness,
I feel the weakness of humanity,
And bow before thee, trembling as I speak.
As our forefather sought to hide himself
From God, when he had sinned, so would I hide
Myself from thee, nor dare to look with eyes
Of sin upon so pure a thing.

SPIRIT.
                        Fear not,
For once like thee I trod, in human shape,
Upon this world of thine. I wandered here

With Israel of old, by night and day,
When Moses and when Aaron led her forth
From the oppressor's land ; and I beheld
The smoky pillar, and the fiery cloud,
And gathered manna at the break of day,
And in the wilderness I died ; and when
They laid my body in the desert sand,
My spirit to another planet soared ;
And there, some time, abode, among the souls
Of those that went before.   From light to light,
From whirling sphere to sphere, since then I've passed,
Each teeming with the souls from other worlds :
In each my due, allotted time I lived ;
In each beheld a purer form of life,
And gained a new degree of holiness ;
In each I learned—*to die is but to live !*
For many times we must be born again
Ere we can hope to see the PERFECT LIGHT ;—
And stars are but the stepping-stones to God.

POET.

O gentle angel ! pause a little while ;
My wildered brain is slow to follow thee
In such illimitable flight of thought.
But, tell me, in these worlds thou speakest of,—
Which seem to our dull eyes as distant specks,
Afar in the blue dome,—if we shall see,

And know the souls we loved upon this earth?—
Once, in the sunny summer of my youth,
I loved a maid, who dreamt not of my love,
Because I told it not, but worshipped her
With silent adoration, day by day ;—
The dearest thought between my soul and God.
But there was one who sought to rival me
In love for her, and hated me ; and him
I hated, with the fiendish hate of hell.
She has been dead to me long years ago ;
But if my soul, in that new life to come,
Where all are equal in the eyes of God,—
Since, with the body, all degrees of rank
And riches die,—should meet hers once again,—
It would be joy indeed, if I might speak
The love in Heaven, I never told on earth.
And he,—I know not if he lives, or where,—
But I would ask forgiveness for the hate
With which I hated him.

SPIRIT.

       Be not deceived.
There are no jealousies in angel life,
Nor is our love the love of flesh and blood ;
Our feelings are not felt in beating hearts,
Nor do we see with eyes half blind with tears ;
But in the special region where we dwell,

We have one feeling, common to us all,—
A spiritual longing for the light
That glows, intensely brightening, star by star,
Upon the wondrous path that leads to God.

POET.

Ah me! do I then learn that all the thoughts,
Which we consider pure and holy here,
Are counted nothing in the life to come?
And are the souls that meet at kissing lips.
And look through loving eyes, transforméd so
That they must meet as strangers after death?

SPIRIT.

Nay! Nay! their recognition is complete,—
For I have watched them meet and seen them smile!

POET.

And do they often visit earth again?

SPIRIT.

Aye, truly!—for the very air we breathe
Is full of spirits, living though unseen,—
The lightning-wingéd messengers of God,

Sent to fulfil His ways to mortal men ;
And thousands of death-liberated souls
Are passing with them to their next abode.

POET.

Oh ! that my love would come to visit me !
Oh ! that the God of Grace would send her down,
From the calm beauty of eternity,
To speak with me, as thou art speaking now !
O blessed spirit ! teach my feeble lips
To form a prayer, that God may suffer me
To see once more that gentle face I loved,
Whose memory still has been the talisman
To cheer the sadness of my failing years.

SPIRIT.

Let not thy frenzied fancy wander thus !
She never can return to thee again
In likeness of the body thou hast loved ;—
For all are changed within the doors of Death.
There flesh and blood must unto dust return,
In the cold darkness of an earthly grave.

POET.

Oh ! I have seen her dead face in my dreams !
Her still pale face, with sad imploring eyes

Beseeching me to come to her,—till I
Have cried aloud, and started from my sleep,
Clasping the vacant air !

SPIRIT.

          And this was nought
But the wild vision of a fevered brain.
Be strong ! the heart of man must needs be strong
To fit his soul for life beyond the grave.

POET.

The strongest here are weak, and full of sin ;
But God will grant it covers many sins
To love a form of His creation so.
Her spirit must have learned to know I loved ;
Yes, after death she must have known it all,
And come too late to look upon my sleep
With steadfast eyes, unutterably sad.

SPIRIT.

The visions thou hast seen are of the flesh,—
For 'tis thy nature to behold in dreams
The strongest images the heart conceives ;
Albeit happy they who see them not,
For punishment must follow fleshly lusts,
Which drag the spirit downward from the light, —
Downward from God.

POET.

Sweet spirit, wrong me not !
There was no dream of lust in all my love.
It was my living soul that sought her soul,
With love of soul for soul, that cannot die :
Such love as mine shall live among the stars
Where time is counted not.

SPIRIT.

This world of thine
Is too remote from God's supreme abode
To nurture love so pure.   The spirit here
By shadows of the flesh is overcast,
The grossness of the body weighs it down,
The passions of the heart are barriers
Between the soul and God.

POET.

The poet's heart
Is moulded fairer by the hand of God
Than hearts of other men.   His soul is like
A star above his life, that leads him on ;
A mirror, which reflects a love divine,
And spreads the truth abroad upon the world.

SPIRIT.

The poets are a precious gift from God,
But they have hearts of simple flesh and blood.
They sing like angels, but they live like men ; *
And when temptations come they also fall.
But once in all the ages of the world,
A child was born whose heart was undefiled.
Of many fierce temptations in the flesh
He stood the test, and over sin and death
He held His way triumphant to the end.
His life was lovely, and His sorrow great,
His cup was bitter, but He murmured not,—
For, at His birth, a star of Love arose,
That shone for men with no uncertain light.
The wise men saw its glory from afar,
And came to worship it—the star of Love.
That came of Love, to lighten all the world.—
And on the hills of Bethlehem that night
The simple shepherds marvelled as they looked,
And heard the grandest anthem ever sung :
The " *Glory ! Glory ! Glory ! unto God,*"
The " *Glory ! in the highest, and on earth
Peace, and goodwill to men,*" by angels sung !
O ! happy, happy shepherds ! to have thus
Foretasted Heaven's music upon earth,

---

* I am indebted to Addison's *Spectator* for the idea contained
in this line.

And one brief moment to have thus beheld
The Glory of the Lord—the Light of Light,
While from their eyes the scales of darkness fell!
And yet men killed Him, for they knew Him not;
And He forgave them of His bounteous love,
And died, in bitter agony, for man,
That man might live for ever after death;
So he would but be faithful and believe.
Oh! what is human love that it should boast,
When matched with His, who died for all the worl!!
The sweetest song, that ever poet sang,
Can bring the poet *nothing* in the end,
If Christ be not the Glory of his soul;—
Therefore, O mortal! let thy sorrow cease,
And weep no more for earthly joys that die;—
Lift up thine eyes unto the Heavens high,
Thy hope is there, lift up, lift up thine heart!

POET.

I know my hope is there, and I have prayed,
With the full passion of a human heart,
For strength to live, and faith to die, and Love
To conquer Death, and freely pass beyond
To that sufficiency of spirit-love,
Which must be all in all.

SPIRIT.

O faithful soul!
Behold in thee His promise is fulfilled;
Look up and listen to the song of those
Whose love has conquered Death—listen and look!

(Song of passing souls.)

We are souls from slumber waking
   Out of darkness into light,
Light of golden Glory breaking
   Far above us in the height.

Far beneath us, dimly rolling,
   Earth retreating we behold;—
Sinking from us,—nor controlling
   Our existence as of old.

Looking back, from far above it,
   Mortal life a sleep doth seem;
All that we remember of it
   Is the shadow of a dream.

Like the sound of many waters,
   Like the voice of thunder, clear,
Songs of angel sons and daughters
   From the golden height we hear.

Some are coming down to meet us,
　Sent to guide us on our way,
With the smile of Peace they greet us
In the light of perfect day.

Far above us, far above us,
　Oh! the glorious song they sing!
And they lead us, for they love us,
　To our Saviour and our King!

SPIRIT.

Lift up thine eyes, and see the beauteous form
Of thy belovéd, whom thou long hast sought;
She comes to guide thee to the living light,
Which is the crown of Life thou shalt receive.

POET.

Oh! I am faint! I cannot draw my breath!
My life is overwhelméd,—Jesus! God!
Sweet Angel! what is this? this sound of song?
This wondrous heavenly music that I hear?

　.　　　.　　　.　　　.

Ah! my beloved child, I see thee now,
I see thy face that I have missed so long!
Stretch out thine arms to me and lift me up,—

For I am very weary of the way,
And let me tell thee I have loved thee long.
Ah ! Love has conquered Death ! I come ! I come !
Belovéd, let me rest my soul on thine !
For I have dwelt in doubt and darkness long ;
But thou wilt lead me, for thou knowest the way,
To God and Home, where it is Perfect Day.

(*Chorus of Angels.*)

God is Love ! O wondrous story !
   God for ever we adore !
Light of Light ! and Lord of Glory !
   Love enthroned for evermore.

(*The morning dawns. The golden sunlight revisits the earth. They find the Poet dead in his chamber ; but his soul has found the soul of his beloved, and hand in hand, rejoicing evermore, they journey onward towards the Perfect Light.*)

MISCELLANEOUS POEMS

THROUGH A GLASS DARKLY.

WHAT do we know?
When all is said and sung,
And all the changes rung,
 What have we got to show?
 We reap the seed we sow,
From Folly's garden sprung.
 What do we know?

What do we know?
When Love we loved is crossed,
And grief must count the cost:
 When tears arise and flow
 From the deep spring of woe,
For Hopes betrayed and lost ;—
 What do we know?

What do we know?
In looking to the height
Of clustered stars at night,

From our sad star below?
Through darkness we must go
Before we see the light,
   Is all we know!

   Yes! all we know!
For standing on the brink
Of Death, from which we shrink,
   The heart must cease to glow,
   And dark the night must grow;
Of Lethe we must drink
   Before we know.

IN THE VALLEY.

O! you are on the sunny height,
  And I am in the valley;
You, where the sky is ever bright,
  And I where shadows dally.
    We met half-way
    One summer day,
And passed an hour light-hearted,
  Then you went up,
  And I came down,
And thus it was we parted.

But often I look up and sigh,
  And pray that God may guide you,
And think of that dear day gone by,
  The day I stood beside you.
    O! pray one prayer,
    Sweetheart, up there,
That, at life's lone finale.
  God's love at last
  May guide me past
The darkness in the valley!

SONG.

COULD we old griefs forget,
  And trials we have met,
And eyes with weeping wet,
    For the bitter woe
    Of Love let go;
Could we take back again
The days we've lived in vain,
Would life have less of pain?
    I do not know!

Can morning dew-drops sweet,
Or the day's noontide heat,
Tell us what we may meet
    In the sunset glow?
    Ah! no! no! no!
We cannot outrun fate,
We must live on and wait,
Till at the ivory gate
    We knock and know!

THE NIGHT OF THE SOUL.

WHEN the faith we have followed
    Has led us astray;
And the cup we have swallowed
    Embittered the way;

When the hope we had trusted
    Has left us to doubt;
And the truth is encrusted
    With canker about;

When our bright star ideal
    Has dropt from the sky;
And the darkness is real
    That answers not why;

When the face that we long for
    Is lost evermore,
And the eyes we did wrong for
    Have ceased to adore;

THE NIGHT OF THE SOUL.

When the tears of our wailing
   Are falling like rain ;
And our prayers unavailing,
   Our pleading in vain ;

When Love to the distance
   His light has withdrawn,
Then Life is existence
   Without any dawn.

And the heart cannot move
   Any nearer the goal ;
For the death of true Love
   Is the night of the soul.

IN SILENCE.

"I'll speak to thee in silence."
—CYMBELINE.

I SPEAK to thee in silence
    When I see the moon arise,
I think thou art beside me
    With a sadness in thine eyes,

Like the night we stood together
    In the dreamland of the past,
And I never broke the silence,
    Though my heart was beating fast.

And I think that thou art near me,
    When I see the stars above,
And I fancy thou canst hear me
    When I tell thee how I love:

And oft I think I hear thy voice,
    Through Heaven's shining bars,
Like whispers of Eternity,
    Among the golden stars.

IN SILENCE

And still of thee I'm dreaming,
  When I lay me down to rest,
As one by one the silent stars
  Are sinking in the west.

I hear thy sweet voice calling,
  "Come where weeping is unknown!"
And I hear the waters falling,
  By the everlasting Throne.

And when the dawn is breaking,
  And the eyes of morn are grey,
Half sleeping, half awaking,
  I am with thee far away.

Where I see thee, faintly smiling,
  On the distant golden shore,
And I speak to thee in silence,
  For I love thee evermore.

SUNSET IN DONEGAL BAY.

THE golden sunset-glow illumed
    The clouds of coming night :
The earth, the air, and sky assumed
    A tranquil holy light.

A painted stillness wrapped the shore,
    And settled over all,
And pictured shadows trembled o'er
    The Bay of Donegal.

The tinted clouds hung glowing o'er
    The islets manifold,
Like fairy draperies flowing o'er
    A phantom sea of gold.

The reeking sun stood half submerged
    In waters far away,
And twilight, softly creeping, verged
    The paths of parting day.

AUTUMN LEAVES.

The autumn leaves lie sere, in the breath
Of the frosty morning air ;
Faded, but beautiful in death :
Once they were green and fair.
   Fading, falling, dying,
   Under the fair blue sky,
   Winds around them sighing.
      " Ye must die ! "

Thus the friends we love and cherish
Leave us one by one ;
As the leaves in autumn perish
When their day is done.
   Failing, fading, dying,
   A voice is ever nigh,
   It whispers, sadly sighing.
      "Ye must die ! "

And some are left till eventide,
To mourn who passed at noon :
Let such with patience still abide,
For they must follow soon.

AUTUMN LEAVES

Weeping, grieving, sighing,
The dead leaves rustle by,
Nature is ever crying,
    " Ye must die."

There will be a bright to-morrow,
Peaceful, painless, fair,
In the land of no more sorrow ;
Dead leaves fall not there !
    God to His own will give
    Sweet rest on high !
    There we shall love and live,
        No more to die !

REQUIESCAT.

" All her bright golden hair
   Tarnished with rust ;
She that was young and fair
   Fallen to dust."
          —OSCAR WILDE.

I STAND beside the new-made grave
Of her I've laid beneath the snow ;
For God has taken what He gave
In love to me a year ago.

Around the old, grey, churchyard gate
The snowdrops grow, and o'er my head
A thrush is singing to its mate ;
For winter with its frost has sped.

And gentle spring is here again,
All nature is rejoicing now ;
My heart alone is full of pain,—
My angel darling, where art thou ?

I try to picture thee afar,
In heaven's spangled vault above,
I think thou art some holy star,
That nightly sheds its light of love.

I thought it were, when thou wert here,
Impossible to love thee more ;
But now thy memory is so dear,
I feel 'twas feeble love I bore.

Why should I wish thee back to me
Again, in such a world as this,
So full of sin and misery,
Where things for ever go amiss ?

I hear thy voice in every wind,
I see thy face in every flower,
Thy thoughts are furrowed in my mind,
And thou art with me every hour.

I feel thy presence ever bright.
A halo that will never die,
As in the tranquil summer night,
The late-set sun still streaks the sky.

The night is short—lo ! eastward far
"Tis red already unto day ;
My morning joy no cloud shall mar,
My heaviness shall pass away.

THE SEASONS OF LIFE.

A MAIDEN in the meadow,
  Plucking flowers to deck her hair
Singing softly as she wanders,
  "Ah! the spring is fresh and fair!"

A listless pair of lovers
  Sitting by the sheltered stream,
O! the golden summer sunshine
  Passing over like a dream!

A chord of memory waking
  A feeble smile which fades,
Ah! sad and sweet is autumn.
  With its chequered lights and shades.

A deathbed sad and solemn,
  And a flood of mourners' tears,
Ah! after weary winter,
  Dawns the spring of endless years.

THE LAST LAY OF A LOCOMOTIVE ENGINE.

TIME is ebbing fast with me,
I shall soon consignéd be
To the limbo land, where locomotives rest ;
But I'll sing before I go,
One Love-strain of long ago,
So posterity may call it a bequest.

It was " Hope " they called my name,
And I brought my driver fame,
For I bore him at an eagle-rushing rate ;
With a clamour and a clang
I for ever, ever sang,
" I'm the unlimited express of fancy freight ! "

And I panted forth a rhyme,
Loud, sonorous and sublime,
And my wheels, in beating time, took a part ;
And the white smoke rolling back
For a furlong o'er the track,
From the furnace-roaring fury of my heart.

On the line a bridge was seen,
  Spanning o'er a deep ravine ;
And I loved it, for the echo of my song,
  Which it echoed as I passed,
  Like a meteor in a blast,
Singing, "'Trust me, fiery lover, I am strong."

And I thought of it at night,
  With enchantment strangely bright,
Like a spiritual flight to Glory's goal ;
  'Not an engine on the line
  Knew the feeling that was mine,
From the sweetness of the fancy in my soul.

But my love was weakly placed,
  And my glory was abased,
For the thing I trusted brought me sorry woe.
  For it fell beneath the strain
  Of my love-impassioned train,
From the sunlight to the dark ravine below.

Then a mist came o'er my eyes ;
  For the splendour of the skies
Had faded, dimly faded from my sight ;
  With an unavailing sob,
  And a great convulsive throb,
My burning heart went out, and all was night.

And I'm now a helpless thing,
Like a bird with broken wing,
Creeping slowly, 'neath a sorrow-laden sky :—
    'Tis the fate of all who trust,
    In a thing as frail as dust,
So to live half broken-hearted, or to die.

ODE TO A SEA-GULL.

Snowy bird on listless wing,
 Pretty thing,
 Hovering
O'er the sun-lit, summer sea ;
Like a happy soul set free
From the burden of its care,
Like a spirit floating fair
 Over there.
As I sit, with careless eye,
I can mark thee passing by,
 Passing nigh ;
In thy passionless unrest
Like a dream-thought half-exprest.
 Being blest !
Does the ceaseless, measured swing
Of the song the surges sing
 Reach thy breast ?
Canst thou read the mystery
 Of the sea ?

When the face of Heaven is fair
    Thou art there ;
But when storm and tempest blow,
Fain would I the haven know
    Where thou dost go.
When the awful wrath of God
    Is abroad ;
When the thunder crashes loud
    From cloud to cloud ;
When the forkéd lightnings flash
Fierce and far, and breakers lash
The rocky shore in desperate wrath,
Casting in the foaming froth
    O'er the land ;
When the rushing mighty wind
Leaps in madness unconfined,
    Wildly grand,—
Rending sails in shattered strips,
Wrecking mariners and ships,
Tossing them in play like chips
    On the strand ;—
Where dost thou for safety flee
From the fury of the sea,
    Seeking peace ?
Tell me of that ocean fair,
Lead me to that haven where
Tempests cease,
At the voice of God, whose will,

Bids the elements be still,
    Whispering " Peace."

Happy bird ! what dost thou know
    Of human woe ?
For thy being has no part
With grief, that rends the human heart.
Beautiful and fair thou art,
    White as snow ;
And thou hearest not my cry,
And thou heedest not my sigh,
Circling now thy course on high
    To the sky ;
Deftly diving down again
    To the main,
The softness of thy breast to lave
    In the wave,
With delicately-tinted feet
    The brine to greet.

O ! if I could soar like thee
    O'er the sea,
    I would flee
Far away and be at rest,
Far across the ocean's breast,
Where the great sun in the west
    Sinks to sleep !

I would melt into the skies,
Where c'ouds of sorrow never rise,
Where the soul's eternal eyes,
    Never weep!

SERENADE FOR THE GUITAR.

I WATCH
      At thy window, my sweet !
      With the moon and the stars overhead,
      By the spirit of love I am led ;
      In the stillness I hear my heart beat :
      I watch, my beloved ! I watch !

As true,
      As the sentinels three *
      Of Aquila, that point to the height,
      Up to Vega, the queen of the night,
      My heart, soul and life look to thee,
      As true, my beloved ! as true !

Good night !
      May thy rest be as still
      As the mist in the vale at my feet,
      And thy slumber as pure and as sweet
      As the moon-glancing dew on the hill ;
      Good night, my beloved ! good night !

   * The three central stars of Aquila point in a line up to Vega
for ever.

Good night !

    May thy dreams be as clear
    As the sanctified light, from afar,
    Of Spica, the virginal star,
    Till the light of the dawn shall appear ;
    Good night, my beloved ! good night !

THE WIND THAT BLOWETH SOFTLY FROM THE SOUTH.

O WIND ! that blowest softly from the South,
To dally round my dear one's dainty face,
To kiss her little, ruby, rose-bud mouth,
And woo her with a delicate embrace,

O ! whisper of the love I bear to her,
And look into her tender eyes, and say
That thou art my most gentle messenger,
To win her heart this sunny, summer day.

And if she blush at mention of my love,
And droop her dark eye-lashes timidly,
Return, as to the ark the faithful dove,
And bring with incensed breath her love to me.

But if she scorn my tenderness, and cast
A haughty look from out a flashing eye,
O ! then return with winter's chilly blast,
And freeze my heart to ice, that I may die !

NEVER AGAIN.

Never again while the years intervene,—
  Long years of weariness, long years of pain;
Never again while the grave lies between
  Us and eternity,—never again
Can we to each other be what we have been,—
  Never again! darling! never again!

Darling, forgive me! for I was to blame,
  I was to blame, but forgive me my share,
My part, in the folly we cannot reclaim;—
  I should have fled when I found you so fair!
But mine was no suddenly-passionate flame,
  Love came upon me like dawn, unaware.

Love, we must linger apart evermore!—
  Hearts, that were blended once, riven in twain;
Sunlight behind us, and shadows before;—
  The sweetness is sipped, and the bitters remain.
All the old yearning and longing of yore
  Blend in the echo—Ah! never again!

SONG.

THE spring was green and lovely,
    The fields were fresh and fair,
And the light of love from Heaven above
    Fell softly everywhere ;
And merrily, in the greenwood tree,
    The wild birds sang their strain ;
And my young heart beat with fulness sweet,
    That will never come back again.

The summer days were golden,
    Sweetly the roses grew ;
And I dreamt one heart, did share a part
    Of the happiness I knew.
As we sat in the shade the pine trees made,
    When the day was nearly done,
And my hopes were bright as the wond'rous light
    Of the slowly sinking sun.

In the still autumn evening
    I sit alone and dream ;

While, like a pall, the shadows fall
   On the sunlight of the stream.
And seared and brown, the leaves float down,
   While the naked boughs remain ;
And the hopes have flown that my heart has known,
   They will never come back again !

SWING SONG.

It soothes my heart-aching
　To swing to and fro,
For the winds are awaking,—
　And freshly they blow
From the cool chambers deep
Of the woods, where they sleep.
And my forehead they kiss,
　Till my cheeks are aglow;
And my senses they steep
In the faintness of bliss,
　As I swing to and fro.

Of Love let me dream
　As I swing to and fro;
For in fancy I seem
　Ever upward to go;
With lightly-shut eyes,
Rocked asleep in the skies.
Oh! could I reveal
　What the lark well must know
As to Heaven he flies,—
That is now what I feel,
　As I swing to and fro!

WHEN THE MYSTIC SCREEN OF NIGHT.

WHEN the mystic screen of night, serene
  Hangs o'er a world of sleep,
And the glancing light of moonbeams bright
  Is mirrored in the deep.

When I gaze on high, in the cloudless sky,
  On countless worlds afar
So pure and fair, in the regions where
  Eternal mysteries are.

The gentle grace of a tender face,
  With thoughts of my loved one come,
Like the trembling beams of a star, that gleams
  Through Heaven's azure dome.

For the stars of night are not more bright
  Than she appears to me :—
The Heavens bare are not more fair,
  For her face is Heavenly.

My dark-eyed maid, in slumber laid,
  Oh ! hear and understand !
And dream of how I love you now
  In sleep's sweet shadow-land.

DREAMLAND VISIONS.

In the twilight of the morning,
    When the day begins to break,
And I lie in conscious slumber,
    Half asleep, and half awake;
When the stars grow dim, dissolving
    In the light of coming day,
Visions glimmer in the distant
    Golden dreamland far away!
        Dreamland visions, floating o'er me,
            Faintly tremble, like a star;
        Loving faces flit before me,
            Smiling on me from afar.

When the dawn, in crimson glory,
    Peeps across the purple hills,
And the song of birds exulting
    All the waking woodland fills;
Then I seem to hear the voices,
    Of the dear ones dead and gone,

Singing from that golden dreamland,
In the cool breath of the dawn.
Singing softly, low, in chorus :
"Ye who patiently await!
Grieve not, grieve no longer for us ;
We have passed the golden gate!"

I MISS YOU.

I MISS you,
Darling, every day!
'Tis hard to hide and put away
The happy thoughts I used to think,
The love that, all unlooked for, grew.
'Tis hard my risen Hope to sink,
And all the joy I had for you.
The precious gem I valued most
Dropt from its setting,—dropt and lost!
You cannot know the pain 'twill cost
To make believe that I forget:
The jewel in my heart was set,
I miss it, darling! every day,
I miss you!

I miss you
When the sun is low,
And clouds reflect the crimson glow;
I miss you through the summer night,
When soft winds sigh and streamlets flow;
When stars o'erhead are shining bright—
Stars that we studied long ago.

D

And when the light of morning gleams
Across the hills, and woods, and streams,
And I awake from happy dreams
 Of days that were, in vanished years ;—
 The sun, uprising, greets my tears.
  By day, by night, I only know
   I miss you !

   I miss you,
  But God's will be done !
  Some grief He gives to every one ;
And some are weak, and some are strong,
 And all must wait His guiding Hand.
The Judge of all can do no wrong !
 His ways I cannot understand ;
But I can pray, and hope, and wait,
That, be it soon, or be it late,
Here, or beyond th' eternal gate,
 You will come back to me again !
 In love, like sunshine after rain.
  His Kingdom come ! His will be done !
   I miss you !

SONNETS

TO VEGA.

I DIMLY can recall what life has been
Before thy transit, my beloved star!
Who broughtest light from where God's angels are.
Have I been dreaming in a distant scene?
Or am I dreaming now, to wake with keen
Remembrance of Love's golden gates ajar?
I cannot read my horoscope afar;
I cannot tell how fate may intervene.

I only know the pain it is to part.—
To long for thee where'er I go abroad!
I love thee with each life-beat of my heart;
And when it beats no more, beneath the sod
My soul must love thee still: because thou art
The purest thought that binds my soul to God.

TO A SISTER STAR.*

ROUND every human heart that glows with heat,
   A host of thoughts in various orbits run,—
   Like planets in their paths around the sun.
Some, like swift Mercury, with busy feet,
The circuit many thousand times complete ;
   While, like dim, distant Neptune, many a one,—
   Its round accomplished,—ages since begun,—
Must sigh, so lone a journey to repeat.

Of all thought-planets, wandering on their way,
   Great Hope, like Jupiter, outweighs the rest ;
O ! may thy planet, Hope, have no dark day !
   I ask the gods to grant me this request :
May no disastrous force arise to stay
   Thee, on thy journey to the golden west.

* Every sympathetic soul is a brother or sister star in the great
eternal race.

BLUE-BELLS

(IN A THICK WOOD).

THE blue-bells raise their heads erect and tall
  Deep in the shadows of this ancient wood,
  Through which the stalwart archer, Robin Hood,
Might have rejoiced to hear his bugle call.
The patient blue-bells flower and fade, though all
  Their days are dark, except when overhead
  The boughs are swayed, and on their mossy bed
The glints of Heaven's sunlight sometimes fall.

How like our day of life this seems to me :—
  For life has gloomy days for all mankind :—
But, as the branches of the darkest tree
  Are sometimes parted by the summer wind,
So Love, when Hope divides the clouds of Care,
May have a passing smile for Life's Despair.

THE ECLIPSE.

WE stood and watched the silver moon arise,
　　Full-orbed and beautiful, that August night;
　　She was so near me I could see the light
Reflected in the Heaven of her eyes.
Then came the shadow, like the swift surprise
　　Of sudden death, stealing upon the bright,
　　Serene face of the silent bride of night;
While stars peeped terror-stricken from the skies.

And then I thought, O happy night thou art!
　　Death cannot steal that silent bride of thine;—
Behold the shadows from her face depart!

　　Unclouded once again we saw her shine;
Only the shadow of another heart
　　Fell with a silent sadness over mine.

THE CONJUNCTION.

Jupiter and Venus.

THROUGH dim-lit regions of the trackless air,
  As I was wandering lonely in the night,
  She came to me, down from the courts of Light,
With Heaven's glory flashing from her hair ;—
God's hand had made no other star so fair.
  I thanked Him for that time of Love's delight,
  Before she left me, weeping for her flight,
And stars were smiling at my heart's despair.

Ah ! Love, that came so near, and could not stay
  To light the lonely path that I have trod !
I will remember thee, and hope, and pray ;
  Till somewhere in the golden fields of God
We meet again, for I can love but thee
Through endless orbits of eternity.

TO ——

THE gay world's friendship is an empty name,
A polished mockery, a hollow sound,
Wherein sincerity is never found:
Wherein Hypocrisy for very shame
Doth hide behind an artificial flame.
True friendship's like a gold mine underground,
Where treasures inexhaustible abound,
Which no one dreams of there, nor seeks to claim;
Save some lone miner, wand'ring on his way,
Who sees a speck upon the surface shine,
And, digging deep, grows richer day by day.
Thy Friendship, O my friend! is such a mine,
Whose wealth I daily better learn to know,
The deeper 'neath the surface that I go.

DREAMING.

DREAMING of song without framing a lay :
  Musing on hopes that remain unexpressed :
  Brooding on music that dwells in the breast :
Thus I sit idling the moments away,
Till at the close of the soft summer day,
  Twilight creeps after the sun to the west.
Dreaming—to dream—I depart to my rest ;
Weary I go, nature's call to obey.
  Then, through the veil that enshadows my sleep,
Voices I hear from a dim, distant shore :—
  Voices that float softly over the deep,
Bidding me sing, how their sorrow is o'er.
  Dreaming, still dreaming, I waken to weep ;—
I am a poet at heart—nothing more !

TO MY PLANET HOPE.

My Planet Hope, evolved from the recess
 Of tracts eternal, in thought's firmament
 When first I hailed thy nebulous advent,
Thy coming magnitude I could not guess;
But when I marked all other stars grow less,
 That in thy presence felt their brightness spent,
My soul stood still to watch the way you went,
Trembling with adoration in excess.

Beloved star, shine on! and shed thy light
 Upon the sin of my idolatry,
Shine on, and I will never call it night
 While thou dost shine, and I have eyes to see!
Were God to call thee suddenly away,
Thus could He strike me blind at bright noonday.

HOME, SWEET HOME.

(*Composed in a Theatre.*)

Amid the loud applause I saw her weep;
  I marked the tears that glistened in her eyes,
  Tears which the gaudy stage could not disguise.
She sang, she felt.   This was emotion deep;
'Twas not the mimic passion, that doth sweep
  But for a moment o'er the soul, and dies
  As suddenly.   I marked, and to my eyes
I felt the unconscious tears of pity creep.

Perchance, in distant, childhood days of yore,
She had a home, that knows her now no more,—
  A home for which she weeps in silence still.
For ever on, from stage to stage to roam,
  Such is the destiny she must fulfil;—
The great cold world is now her only home.

TO ——.

Rich in simplicity of girlish grace,
.O happy maid ! I love to watch thy ways !—
Sweet to my fancy is thy bright child-face,
And my thoughts follow thee from place to place,
So I forget to count the hours and days.
All I can do—to meditate and gaze.
Unbidden fancies run an idle race,
Near thee my heart no argument obeys.
Deep in the shadows of thy dark brown eyes,—
Eyes full of truth, that scarce conceal a thought,
Regions of tranquil light, like summer skies
Seen in the deep, blue midnight, star-inwrought,—
Oft have I looked, and silently adored ;—
No fairer view the heavenly fields afford !

FRIENDSHIP.

THE days of careless youth have passed away :
  The circling years have brought us face to face
With sterner, unromantic truths to-day.
  No longer Pleasure's butterflies we chase,
As in the sunshine, when our life was May.
Friendship alone remains without a trace
Of Time's destroying hand. We struggle on
Through the uncertain mist, which lies before ;—
The past we never, never can restore.
  We never more can look with love upon
  The faces of the dear ones, who have gone
To rest, "in that calm, solemn, spirit-land."
But, with the smile of friendship, hand in hand
  We face the days we could not face alone.

SPRING.

THE Spring in beauty decks the glen once more.
   Moving mysteriously from day to day ;
   The trees in robes of green their boughs array ;
The stream forgets its angry winter roar ;
And birds, in ecstasy, new-mated, pour
   Through all the woods a merry roundelay.
   Through the tall pines the zephyr woos its way,
And whispers to the beech and sycamore.

And gently moves my mountain maid divine,
   As though the Spring went with her everywhere.
O ! that the zephyr's listless ways were mine,
   That I, as unobtrusively, might dare
To urge my pleading at her sacred shrine,
   And woo my Goddess in her temple there !

TO AUTUMN.

AH ! linger with me yet a little while,
　For I have loved thy beauty day by day.
　My yearning heart would have thee ever stay;
For like a blushing maid thou dost beguile
My fancy, with thy rosy-dimpled smile.
　Oh ! that I now might clasp thy hands, and say,
　" I love thee, thou must never go away !"—
But thou art going, and my words are vain.

Go, autumn, go ! thy glories are but laid
　To rest awhile ; they will return again !
But never more beneath thy happy shade
　Shall Love return to me ; for bitter pain
Hath killed the hopes I cherished : they depart,—
And winter's chilly breath benumbs my heart.

THE LAST NIGHT.

A DREAM.

BESIDE a mighty forest, far outspread,
　　I stood in darkness, near life's utmost end.
　　When lo ! a sound arose, that seemed to rend
The heart of all the world.　Earth's bosom bled
From mountain peaks behind me, flaming red.
　　Then through the darkness, hurriedly, you came,
　　And fainted in my arms, who called your name ;
Pale, like the ghost of one already dead.

There, at the end of Earth and Life, I knelt
　　In tears, and kissed your silent lips ; and you
Awoke, with eyes of wonder wide.　I felt
　　Your spirit shudder, and I knew *you knew* !
For like a soul that Death could never kill,
You looked and smiled, and left me dreaming still.